THE MAGIC NUTCRACKER

Modern Curriculum Press
BEGINNING TO READ Series

THE MAGIC NUTCRACKER

Margaret Hillert

Illustrated by Portia Iversen

MODERN CURRICULUM PRESS
Cleveland • Toronto

Library of Congress Cataloging in Publication Data

Hillert, Margaret.
The magic nutcracker.

SUMMARY: When a young girl rescues her nutcracker from an attack by mice, the nutcracker becomes a prince and takes her to see the Snow King and Queen, the Sugar Plum Fairy, and waltzing flowers.
[1. Fairy tales] I. Iversen, Portia. II. Title
PZ8.H5425Mag [E] 80-13667

ISBN 0-8136-5574-9 (Paperback)
ISBN 0-8136-5074-7 (Hardcover)

5 6 7 8 9 10 89

Library of Congress Catalog Card Number: 80-13667

Is this for me?
It looks like a little man.
What is it for?

Oh, I see.
I can make it work.
And I will have something
good to eat.

Now I have to go.
I like you, little man,
but you can not come with me.

Oh, my. Oh, my.
I want my little man.
I will get up and
go look for it.

Oh, oh, oh.
What is this?
What is this?
I do not like it.

My little man is down.
This is not good.
How can I help?

Go away.
Go away.
See what I can do
to you.

O - o - o - h!
How did you do that?
You are not little now.
You are a big man.

Yes, I am big now.
And I like you.
I want you to go with me.
I want you to see something.

Now come with me.
Get into this.
It will take us away.

Look at this.
Oh, look at this.
See how pretty it is.

And look who is here.
Guess who.
Can you guess who it is?

Away we go.
Away, away.
What will we find out here?

Here is a girl.
A pretty, pretty girl.
She wants us to come in.

See what she can do.
She is good at it.
We can do it, too.

Oh, my. Oh, my.
Look at this
and this
and this!

We can eat it.
It is good, good, good.
Oh, I like it here!

And what have we here?
Something pretty.
Red, yellow, blue.

Come now.
Come with me.
We have to go.
Away, away we go.

Here you are.
Get in. Get in.
I have to go now.

This is funny.
How did I get here?
And how did you get here?
Now you are little.
That is good.
I like you this way.

Margaret Hillert, author of several books in the MCP Beginning-To-Read Series, is a writer, poet, and teacher.

The Magic Nutcracker uses the 66 words listed below.

a
am
and
are
at
away

big
blue
but

can
come

did
do
down

eat

find
for
funny

get
girl
go
good
guess

have
help
here
how

I
in
into
is
it

like
little
look(s)

make
man
me
my

not
now

oh
out

pretty

red

see
she
something

take
that
this
to
too

up
us

want(s)
way
we
what
who
will
with
work

yellow
yes
you